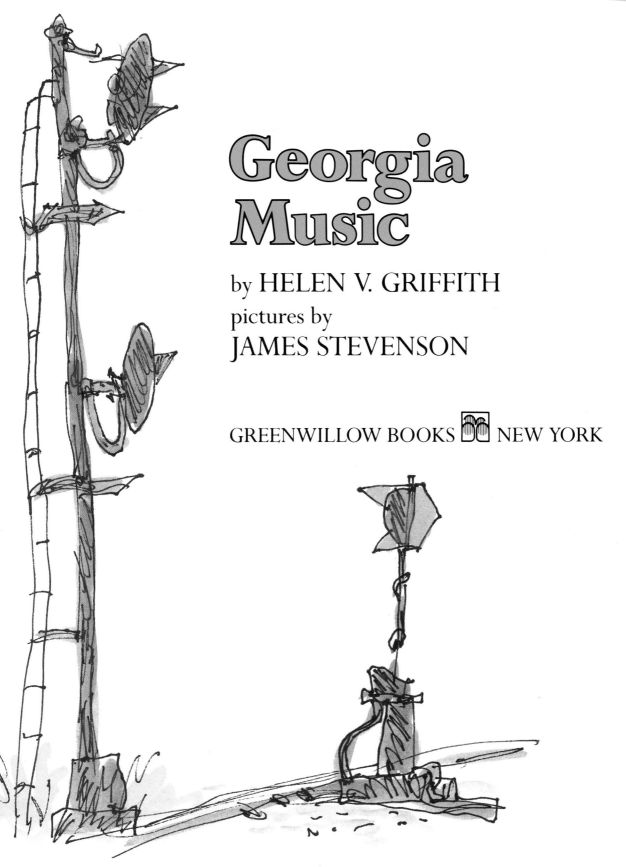

# Georgia Music

by HELEN V. GRIFFITH

pictures by
JAMES STEVENSON

GREENWILLOW BOOKS  NEW YORK

**FOR SUSAN,**
**WHO KNOWS HER OWN MIND**

The full-color art was
prepared as black line
with watercolor paints.
The typeface is Perpetua.

Greenwillow Books,
a division of William
Morrow & Company, Inc.,
105 Madison Avenue,
New York, N.Y. 10016.

Printed in Hong Kong by
South China Printing Co.
First Edition
10 9 8 7 6 5 4 3 2 1

Library of Congress
Cataloging-in-Publication Data
Griffith, Helen V.
Georgia music.
Summary:
A little girl and her grandfather
share two different kinds of
music, that of his mouth organ
and that of the birds and
insects around his cabin.
[1. Grandfathers—Fiction.
2. Music—Fiction.
3. Nature—Fiction]
I. Stevenson, James, (date) ill.
II. Title.
PZ7.G8823Ge   1986
[E]       85-24918
ISBN 0-688-06071-4
ISBN 0-688-06072-2 (lib. bdg.)

An old man lived by himself in a cabin near the railroad tracks in the state of Georgia.

He spent his winters doing odd jobs and watching the trains go by and thinking about old times.

But as soon as it was spring he put on his straw hat, pulled his hoe out from under the porch, and chopped out a good-sized patch of garden beside the cabin. Then all summer long he worked in that garden, growing collards and melons and black-eyed peas.

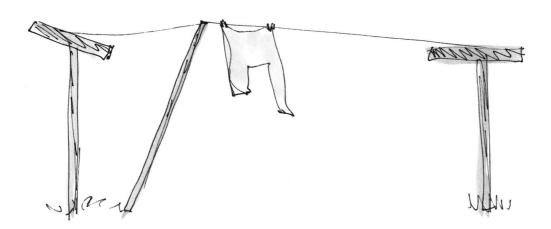

One summer the old man's daughter took the
train from Baltimore to Georgia for a visit, and she took
her own daughter along with her. After a few days she
had to get back to Baltimore, but she left the girl there
with her grandfather for the whole long summer.

The old man never said how he felt about that, but
he didn't seem to mind. The girl didn't mind either. She
liked it right away. She liked the hot garden patch with
its green rows of seedlings, and she liked the little cabin
that shook when the trains thundered by. When she
stopped being shy of her grandfather she liked him, too.
She followed him around his garden while he worked,
and sometimes she stepped on the little green seedlings,
but if the old man noticed, he never said anything.

He found her an old straw hat and a hoe that wasn't too heavy and showed her how to chop weeds. It was hard work, and at first she was clumsy at it, but the old man said he didn't know how he'd ever done without her.

They would work all morning, their hoes going chink, chink up and down the rows, while a mockingbird flew from fence post to fence post, flapping his wings and singing noisy songs at them.

"Sassy old bird," the man would say, and the girl would say it, too, "Sassy old bird," and they would look at each other and laugh out loud.

At noon they sat under a tree and ate their lunch, and then they would lie back on the grass and rest. The old man would pull his straw hat over his face, and the girl would make a pillow out of hers and lie looking up at the leaves and the sky.

It was so quiet that they could hear the leaves touching each other, and the bumblebees bumbling, and the crickets and grasshoppers whirring and scratching. And every now and then the old man would nod his head under his straw hat and say, "Now, that's music."

Then they would go to sleep under the tree while the summer sounds went on and on in their ears and in their brains.

In the evenings the two of them sat out on the rickety porch steps and the old man played tunes on his mouth organ. He knew a lot of songs and he taught the words to the girl so she could sing with the music.

The old man said he was really playing for the crickets and the grasshoppers because they made music for him in the daytime. He said they liked it, and the girl thought so, too.

At night they went to sleep hearing the katydids and the tree frogs and the chuck-will's-widows singing and singing, and some nights the mockingbird called nearly all night long. Then the girl would smile to herself and whisper, "Sassy old bird."

When September came the girl didn't want to go home and she could see that her grandfather was sorry, too. Her mother promised that she could come back next summer, and they had to be satisfied with that.

But the next summer wasn't the same.

The girl and her mother knew something was wrong as soon as they saw the cabin. Weeds were growing through the steps and a wild rosebush had almost taken over the porch. They found the old man sitting in a chair with a quilt over his lap and his eyes closed.

"I ain't sick," he told them. "Just mighty tired."
But they closed up the cabin and took him back with
them to Baltimore. The girl knew he was sicker than he
said or he never would have gone.

There was nothing wrong with their home in
Baltimore, but the old man wasn't happy there. He sat
in a chair looking worried and sad, and the girl knew he
was thinking of the old cabin and the garden that didn't
get planted that year.

She tried to talk to him, but nothing seemed to
interest him, and it just wasn't like it had been in
Georgia.

One day the girl got out the old man's mouth organ and put it in his hand.

"Play me a tune, Grandaddy," she said, but he just held the mouth organ in his hand and looked at it.

The girl took it back and put her lips on it and blew, and when the old man heard the sound his eyes opened wide and he looked right at her, something he never did anymore.

So she made more sounds come out of the mouth organ, and then she began blowing in and out, finding out how it worked, and at last she was able to play a little tune on it.

"Did you like that, Grandaddy?" she asked, but she already knew he did.

From then on the girl sat with her grandfather every day and practiced playing the mouth organ until she began to be good at it. She taught herself all the old songs her grandfather had played for her, and she played them over and over.

One day, after she had played everything she knew, she found herself playing a different kind of music and making up brand new songs. Except it wasn't exactly music and they weren't real songs. They were the sounds she remembered from that Georgia summer— cricket chirps and tree frog trills and bee buzzes and bird twitters.

She shut her eyes and swayed back and forth and she could almost feel the hot sun on her back and the hoe handle in her hands, and for a while it was like being right back in Georgia.

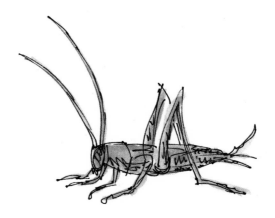

Then the old man gave a little chuckle and the girl heard him whisper to himself, "Sassy old bird." So she said it, too, "Sassy old bird."

And then the girl and her grandfather looked at each other and laughed out loud.